Geronimo Stilton

ENGLISH!

1 NUMBERS AND COLOURS 數字和顏色

新雅文化事業有限公司
www.sunya.com.hk

Geronimo Stilton English
NUMBERS AND COLOURS 數字和顏色

作　　者：Geronimo Stilton 謝利連摩・史提頓
譯　　者：Phoebe Wong
責任編輯：王燕參
封面繪圖：Giuseppe Facciotto
插圖繪畫：Claudio Cernuschi, Andrea Denegri, Daria Cerchi
內文設計：Angela Ficarelli, Raffaella Picozzi
出　　版：新雅文化事業有限公司
香港筲箕灣耀興道3號東匯廣場9樓
營銷部電話：（852）2562 0161
客戶服務部電話：（852）2976 6559
傳真：（852）2597 4003
網址：http://www.sunya.com.hk
電郵：marketing@sunya.com.hk
發　　行：香港聯合書刊物流有限公司
香港新界大埔汀麗路36號中華商務印刷大廈3字樓
電話：（852）2150 2100　傳真：（852）2407 3062
電郵：info@suplogistics.com.hk
印　　刷：C & C Offset Printing Co.,Ltd
香港新界大埔汀麗路36號
版　　次：二〇一一年二月初版
10 9 8 7 6 5 4 3 2 1

Original title: NUMERI E COLORI
Based upon an original idea by Elisabetta Dami
www.geronimostilton.com

9/F, Eastern Central Plaza, 3 Yiu Hing Rd, Shau Kei Wan, Hong Kong
Published and printed in Hong Kong

CONTENTS
目錄

BENJAMIN'S CLASSMATES
班哲文的老師和同學們

Maestra Topitilla
托比蒂拉・德・托比莉斯

Rarin
拉琳

Diego
迪哥

Rupa
露芭

Tui
杜爾

David
大衛

Sakura
櫻花

Mohamed
穆哈麥德

Tian Kai
田凱

Oliver
奧利佛

Milenko
米蘭哥

Trippo
特里普

Carmen
卡敏

Atina
阿提娜

Esmeralda
愛絲梅拉達

Pandora
潘朵拉

Takeshi
北野

Kuti
菊花

Benjamin
班哲文

Hsing
阿星

Laura
羅拉

Kiku
奇哥

Antonia
安東妮婭

Liza
麗莎

GERONIMO AND HIS FRIENDS

謝利連摩和他的家鼠朋友們

謝利連摩・史提頓 Geronimo Stilton

一個古怪的傢伙，簡直可以說是一隻笨拙的文化鼠。他是《鼠民公報》的總裁，正花盡心思改變報紙業的歷史。

菲・史提頓 Tea Stilton

謝利連摩的妹妹，她是《鼠民公報》的特派記者，同時也是一個運動愛好者。

班哲文・史提頓 Benjamin Stilton

謝利連摩的小侄兒，常被叔叔稱作「我的小乳酪」，是一隻感情豐富的小老鼠。

潘朵拉・華之鼠 Pandora Woz

柏蒂・活力鼠的小侄女、班哲文最好的朋友，是一隻活潑開朗的小老鼠。

柏蒂・活力鼠 Patty Spring

美麗迷人的電視新聞工作者，致力於她熱愛的電視事業。

賴皮 Trappola

謝利連摩的表弟，非常喜歡食物，風趣幽默，是一隻饞嘴、愛開玩笑的老鼠，善於將歡樂傳遞給每一隻鼠。

麗萍姑媽 Zia Lippa

謝利連摩的姑媽，對鼠十分友善，又和藹可親，只想將最好的給身邊的鼠。

艾拿 Iena

謝利連摩的好朋友，充滿活力，熱愛各項運動，他希望能把對運動的熱誠傳給謝利連摩。

史奎克・愛管閒事鼠 Ficcanaso Squitt

謝利連摩的好朋友，是一個非常有頭腦的私家偵探，總是穿着一件黃色的乾濕褸。

HELLO!　你好！

親愛的小朋友，很高興你選擇和我一起學習英語。

不用擔心，跟我一起來，你會發現學習英語原來是這麼簡單和好玩的！你仍然有點擔心？讓我告訴你一個秘密吧：班哲文、潘朵拉也和你一樣，你還有什麼好擔心的呢？

與他們一起來，你將會進入一個充滿樂趣的遊戲世界，很快你就會知道如何用英語說出不同物件的名稱，它們的數量有多少，還有它們是什麼顏色的！

在我們開始之前，讓我先來介紹一下自己吧。

A SONG FOR YOU!

Hello!

Hello! Hello!
Hello, hello, hello...
my name's Stilton,
Geronimo Stilton!

跟我謝利連摩．史提頓一起學英文，
就像玩遊戲一樣簡單好玩！

你可以一邊看着圖畫一邊讀。
以下有幾個標誌，你要特別留意：

當看到 標誌時，你可以聽CD，一邊聽，一邊跟着朗讀，還可以跟着一起唱歌。

當看到 標誌時，你可以和朋友們一起玩遊戲，或者嘗試回答問題。題目很簡單，它們對鞏固你所學過的內容很有幫助。

當看到 標誌時，你要注意看一下格子裏的生字，反覆唸幾遍，掌握發音。

最後，不要忘記完成小測驗和練習冊裏的問題！看看你有多聰明吧。

祝大家學得開開心心！

謝利連摩．史提頓

TOYS 玩具

妙鼠城一個寧靜的下午，班哲文和潘朵拉放學後，我帶他們一起去瑪思卡波姑丈的玩具店逛逛。到了玩具店，瑪思卡波姑丈笑着歡迎我們，並親切地和我們打招呼。班哲文和潘朵拉也和瑪思卡波姑丈打招呼。

這裏有些什麼玩具？一起跟班哲文和潘朵拉用英語說說這些玩具的名稱吧！

toy	玩具
toys	toy的眾數
shop	商店
shops	shop的眾數

A SONG FOR YOU!

Track 2

Toys

A ball
a car
a bicycle
a plane
a skateboard
a puzzle
and... a train!

1. 班哲文和潘朵拉分別最喜歡哪一種玩具？仔細觀察下面的圖畫，然後用英語說出它們的名稱。

The bicycle!

The skateboard!

2. 你最喜歡的玩具是什麼？用英語說出來。
3. 謝利連摩帶來了一個大箱子，你知道裏面裝的是什麼嗎？想知道的話，趕快翻到第13頁吧。

答案：
1. 班哲文最喜歡的玩具是：the bicycle, the ball, the car, the plane; 潘朵拉最喜歡的玩具是：the skateboard, the doll, the skipping rope, the train.

NUMBERS 數字

瑪思卡波姑丈拿出一個箱子給我們看，誰知剛一打開，一個個五顏六色的皮球就從箱子裏滾出來。不一會兒，皮球滾得遍地都是。七彩繽紛的皮球在班哲文和潘朵拉的身邊滾動着、跳躍着，和他們玩捉迷藏的遊戲呢，頓時令整間店子充滿了歡笑聲。班哲文和潘朵拉一邊數，一邊收集滿地奔跑的皮球。你也一起用英語數數這些皮球吧！

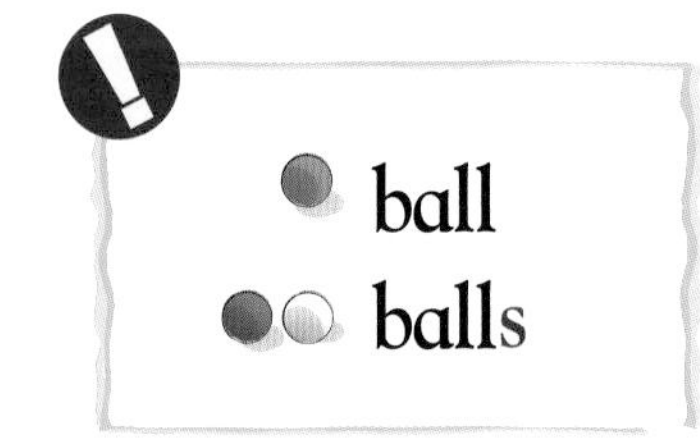

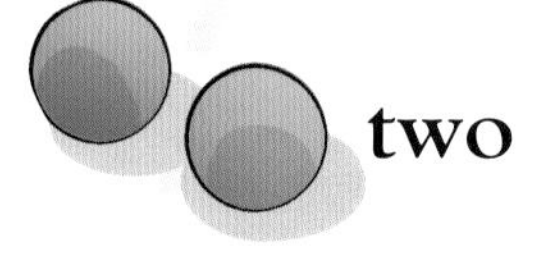

three

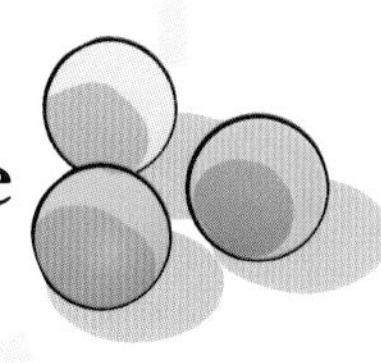

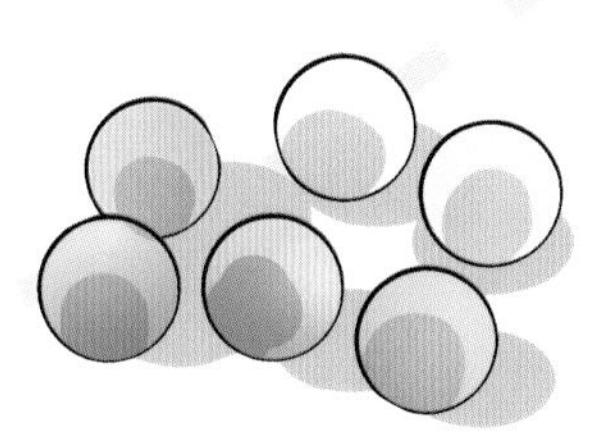

six

A SONG FOR YOU!

Ten Balls

One ball, two balls,
three balls, four.
Five balls, six balls,
seven balls.
Eight balls, nine balls,
ten balls
and stop!

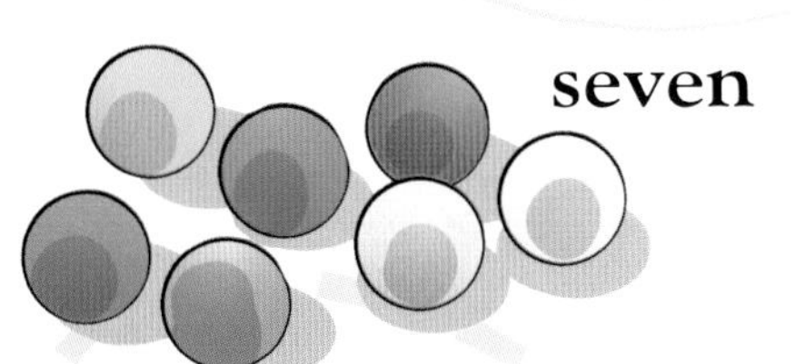

seven

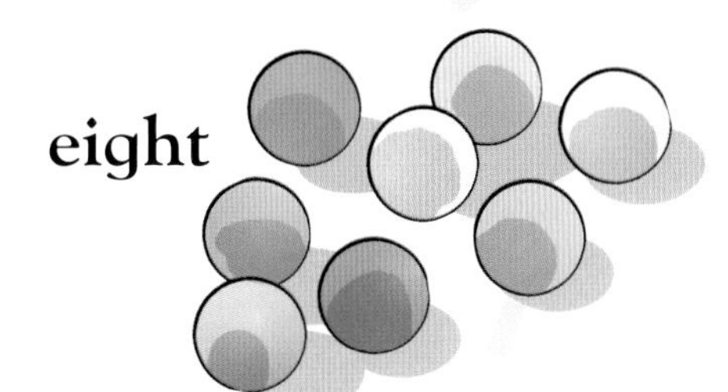

eight

nine

0 zero
1 one ball
2 two balls
3 three balls
4 four balls
5 five balls
6 six balls
7 seven balls
8 eight balls
9 nine balls
10 ten balls

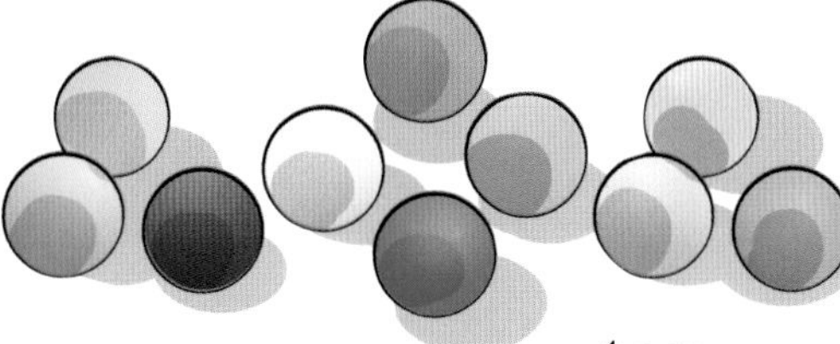

ten

✪ 你也跟着一起用英語唱這首歌吧！

IN THE BOX 在箱子裏

就在班哲文和潘朵拉玩得正高興的時候，一輛滿載着箱子的貨車來到玩具店前，準備卸下玩具。這時，菲剛好也來到玩具店，她幫助他們打開箱子，把那些簇新的玩具拿出來，並整理和擺放好。

這些新玩具有什麼呢？它們的數量各有多少？請你跟着班哲文和潘朵拉一起來數一數，並用英語說出來吧。

... rocking horse

... dolls

... cars

... lorries

... planes

... videogames

答案：
one rocking horse, four dolls, six cars, five lorries, three planes, two videogames.

MY TOYS 我的玩具

班哲文和潘朵拉高興地交換着玩具，最後，他們都得到了自己喜歡的玩具。看，班哲文和潘朵拉正在說什麼呢？你也跟着他們一起用英語說說吧。

my bicycle

my plane

my ball

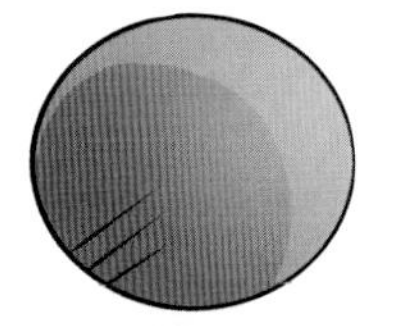

my car

my skateboard

my doll

my train

my skipping rope

這時，謝利連摩打開了箱子，現在你知道箱子裏面裝的是什麼了吧！試着用英語說出來。

my	我的
Wow!	哇！（表示驚訝）
Great!	太好了！

答案：ten kites

COLOURS 顏色

小朋友看到箱子裏放着的是風箏，都感到十分驚喜！我帶着班哲文、潘朵拉和其他小朋友來到郊外放風箏，他們一邊玩耍，一邊用英語說出風箏的顏色，你也趕快加入他們吧！

★ 班哲文和潘朵拉的風箏分別是什麼顏色的？試着用英語說出來。

答案：班哲文的風箏的顏色：blue;
潘朵拉的風箏的顏色：green.

LET'S PLAY "GERONIMO SAYS..." 一起來玩「謝利連摩說……」

現在，我要跟大家玩一個遊戲，你和你的朋友也可以一起參加。這個遊戲叫做「謝利連摩說……」請仔細聽聽我的命令，然後找出相應的圖畫。

Geronimo says...
Touch something red!

我不停地變換着命令，請你用英語重複說出我的命令，並找出相應的圖畫。

Touch something yellow!

Touch something green!

Touch something orange!

Touch something blue!

COLOURFUL KITES
色彩繽紛的風箏

我忽然記起自己小時候也很喜歡放風箏，於是馬上為大家演奏了一首關於放風箏的歌，你也跟着班哲文、潘朵拉和其他小朋友一起唱吧。

✪ 這裏有四隻風箏沒有飛上天，試着用英語説出它們的顏色。

答案：沒有飛上天的風箏的顏色是：black, white, purple, brown.

A SONG FOR YOU!

Track 4

Kites

A red kite
a blue kite
a yellow kite
an orange kite
fly high in the sky!

My red kite
my blue kite
my yellow kite
my orange kite
fly high in the sky!

A green kite
a pink kite
my yellow kite
my orange kite
fly high in the sky!
Fly high in the sky!

!

a red kite
一隻紅色的風箏

a yellow kite
一隻黃色的風箏

IS... ARE... 是……

班哲文、潘朵拉和他們的朋友們一起玩耍，每個人都找到了自己喜歡的玩具，他們想用英語描述自己的玩具是什麼顏色的，但這些玩具中哪些該用動詞「is」（主語是單數時用），哪些該用動詞「are」（主語是眾數時用）呢？

仔細觀察每幅圖畫，然後用英語說出每種玩具的顏色，完成句子。

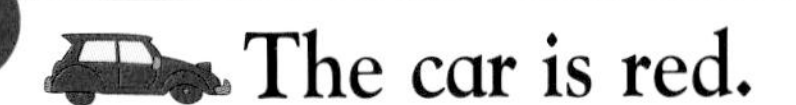
The car is red.

這輛汽車是紅色的。

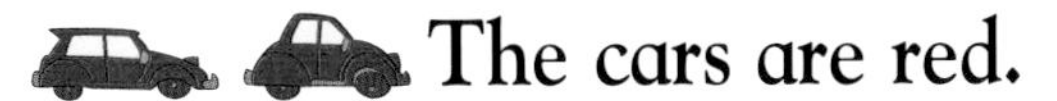
The cars are red.

這些汽車是紅色的。

My car is red.

我的汽車是紅色的。

My cars are red.

我的汽車是紅色的。

My teddy bear is ...

My rollerblades are ...

My plane is ...

My rocking horse is ... and ...

My train is ... and ...

My bicycle is ...

My videogame is ... and ...

My doll is ...

〈送給賴皮的玩具〉

賴皮今天很高興，因為今天是他的生日！

菲：賴皮，你看起來很開心呢！

賴皮：看，這麼多禮物，全是送給我的！

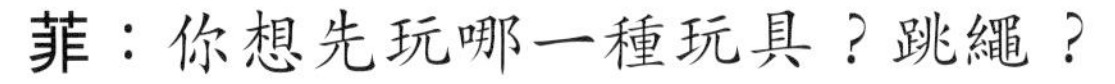

菲：你想先玩哪一種玩具？跳繩？

賴皮：不！這太簡單了！

菲：你想試試你的滾軸溜冰鞋嗎？

賴皮：不！這太容易了……

班哲文：那試試你的滑板車吧！

賴皮：不！這太沉悶了！

賴皮：我想嘗試玩滑板。

Here is Trappola on his
skateboard. He can balance...

賴皮正在玩他的滑板。他能夠保持平衡……

He can slalom...
I'm very good!

他能夠轉動自如地前進，避過一些障礙……

賴皮：我的技術不錯吧！

He jumps and...
I can fly!

他跳起來了，然而……

賴皮：我飛起來了！

...he falls!
Ouch!
It hurts...

……他跌倒了！

賴皮：哎唷！很痛啊……

班哲文：他的鼻子受傷了！
潘朵拉：噢，可憐的賴皮！

潘朵拉：你還好嗎，賴皮？
賴皮：嗯……我沒事，謝謝！

班哲文：玩滑板真是不簡單，不容易，也不會令人感到沉悶……
菲：但你必須多多練習，賴皮！

賴皮：好主意！那我現在開始練習玩滑板車了！

TEST 小測驗

1. 用英語說出下面玩具的名稱。

2. 用英語說出下面的顏色。

3. 用英語說出下面的短語。

我的皮球 *my...*	我的洋娃娃 *my...*	我的滾軸溜冰鞋 *my...*	我的玩具 *my...*

4. 數一數下列各圈中有小汽車多少輛，然後用英語說出來。

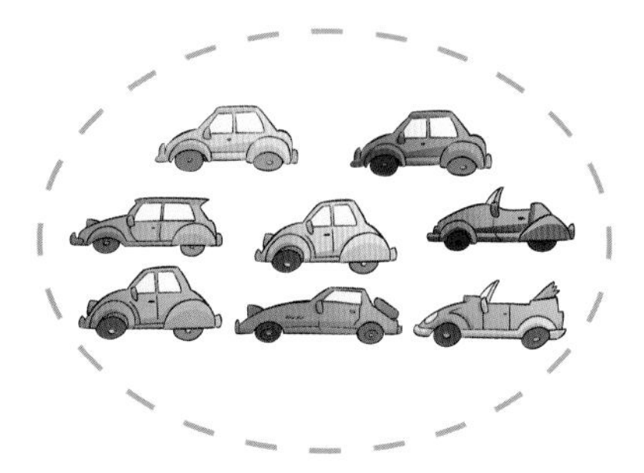

5. 用英語說出下面的句子。

(a) 我的球是紅色的。
My ball is...

(b) 我的滑板車是黃色的。
My scooter is...

(c) 我的滾軸溜冰鞋是藍色的。
My... are...

(d) 我的火車是綠色和黃色的。
... ... is ... and ...

(英、粵、普發聲)

DICTIONARY 詞典

A

and 和

B

balance 平衡

ball 皮球

bicycle 單車

birthday 生日

black 黑色

blue 藍色

boring 沉悶

box 箱子

brown 棕色

C

can 能夠

car 汽車

D

doll 洋娃娃

domino 多米諾骨牌

E

easy 容易

eight 八

F

fall 跌倒

five 五

fly 飛

four 四

G

good 好

green 綠色

H

happy 高興

hello 你好

here 這裏

high 高

his 他的

hurt 受傷

I

idea 主意

J

jump 跳

K

kite 風箏

L

look 看

lorry 貨車

M

my 我的

N

name 名字

nine 九

nose 鼻子

O

one 一

orange 橙色

P

pink 粉紅色

plane 飛機

play 玩

poor 可憐

practice 練習

present 禮物

purple 紫色

puzzle 拼圖

R

red 紅色

rocking horse 搖木馬

rollerblades 滾軸溜冰鞋

S

say 說

scooter 滑板車

seven 七

shop 商店

simple 簡單

six 六

skateboard 滑板

skipping rope 跳繩

sky 天空

slalom 轉動自如地前進

start 開始

stop 停止

swing 鞦韆

T

teddy bear 玩具熊

ten 十

thank you 謝謝

three 三

today 今天

touch 觸摸

toy 玩具

toy shop 玩具店

train 火車

try 嘗試

two 二

V

videogame 電子遊戲

W

want 想

white 白色

Y

yellow 黃色

your 你的

Z

zero 零

親愛的小朋友，你學得開心嗎？很開心，對不對？好極了！你有沒有覺得學英語很簡單呢？很快你就能夠說流利的英語了。我等着你下次繼續跟班哲文和潘朵拉一起玩一起學英語呀。現在要說再見了，當然是用英語說啦！

Goodbye! Bye-bye!
Bye-bye!

Bye-bye!
Goodbye!
Goodbye!
Bye-bye!
Bye-bye!

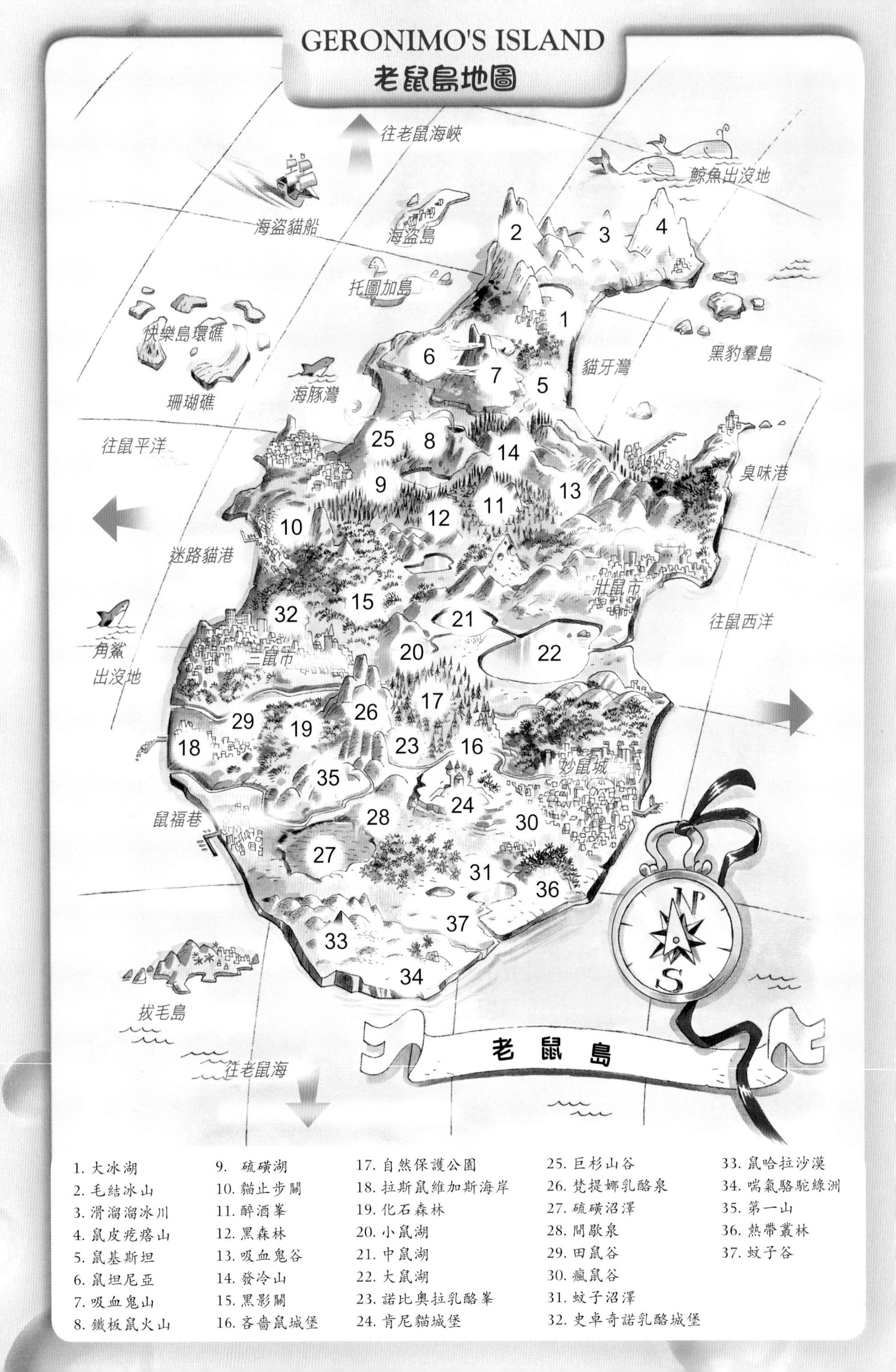
GERONIMO'S ISLAND
老鼠島地圖
往老鼠海峽
鯨魚出沒地
海盜貓船
海盜島
托圖加島
快樂島環礁
珊瑚礁
海豚灣
貓牙灣
黑豹羣島
往鼠平洋
臭味港
迷路貓港
壯鼠市
往鼠西洋
角鯊
出沒地
三鼠市
妙鼠城
鼠福巷
拔毛島
往老鼠海
老鼠島
1. 大冰湖
2. 毛結冰山
3. 滑溜溜冰川
4. 鼠皮疙瘩山
5. 鼠基斯坦
6. 鼠坦尼亞
7. 吸血鬼山
8. 鐵板鼠火山
9. 硫磺湖
10. 貓止步關
11. 醉酒峯
12. 黑森林
13. 吸血鬼谷
14. 發冷山
15. 黑影關
16. 吝嗇鼠城堡
17. 自然保護公園
18. 拉斯鼠維加斯海岸
19. 化石森林
20. 小鼠湖
21. 中鼠湖
22. 大鼠湖
23. 諾比奧拉乳酪峯
24. 肯尼貓城堡
25. 巨杉山谷
26. 梵提娜乳酪泉
27. 硫磺沼澤
28. 間歇泉
29. 田鼠谷
30. 瘋鼠谷
31. 蚊子沼澤
32. 史卓奇諾乳酪城堡
33. 鼠哈拉沙漠
34. 喘氣駱駝綠洲
35. 第一山
36. 熱帶叢林
37. 蚊子谷

Geronimo Stilton

EXERCISE BOOK

練習冊

想知道自己對 NUMBERS AND COLOURS 掌握了多少，
趕快打開後面的練習完成它吧！

ENGLISH!

1 NUMBERS AND COLOURS 數字和顏色

TOYS 玩具

✪ 把下面每幅圖的虛線連起來，看看圖中畫的是什麼。然後把字母重新排列好，在橫線上寫出它們的英文名稱。

1.

r a c

____

2.

o y r l r

____

3.

b c l i y c e

____

4.

o c s o e t r

____

WHAT'S MISSING?

缺少了什麼？

✪ 下面的圖畫都缺少了一部分，你能猜出它們是什麼嗎？根據提示，在橫線上寫出它們的名稱。

提示：

teddy bear
rocking horse
kite
plane
skateboard

1.

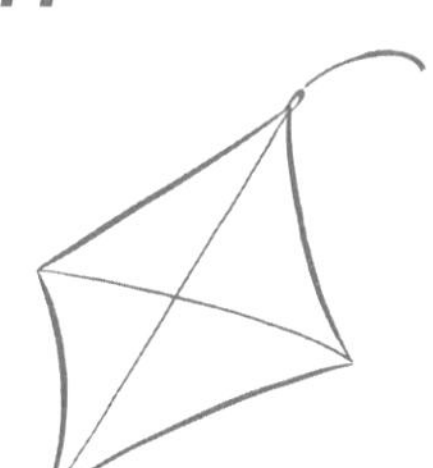

____

2.

____

3.

____

4.

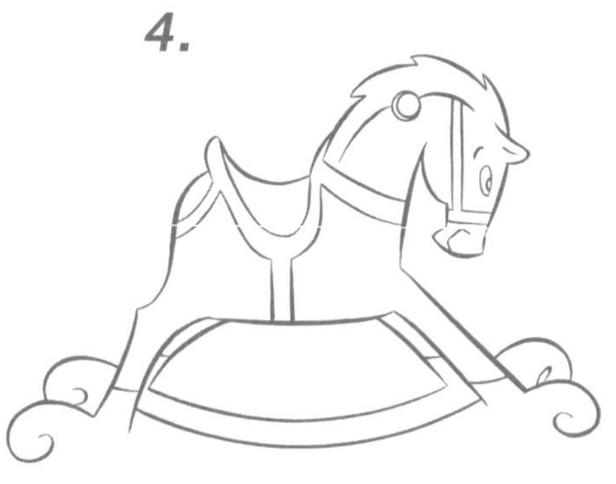

____

5.

____

MY TRAIN 我的火車

✪ 根據火車上標示的顏色，把火車填上顏色。

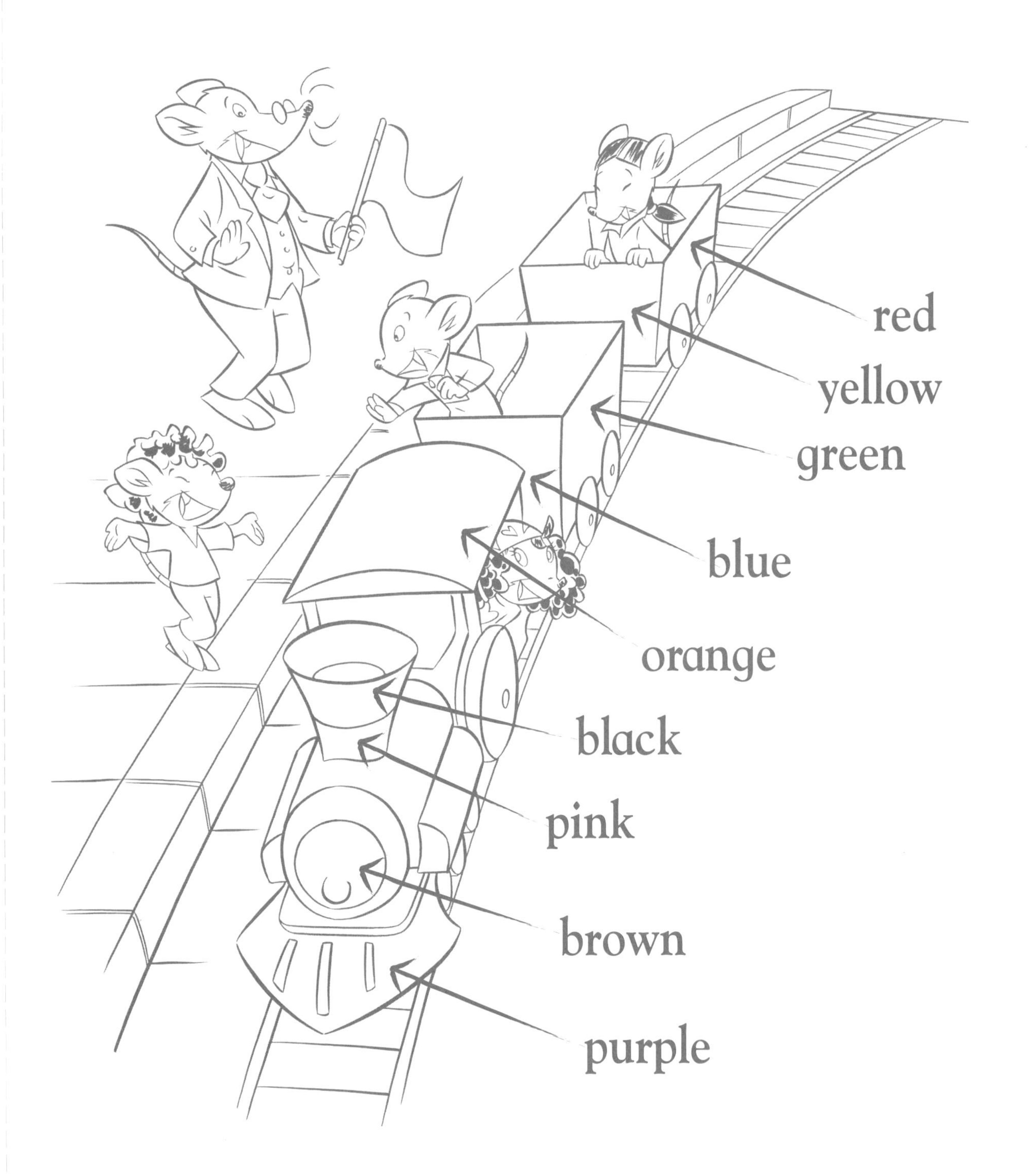

KITES　風箏

✪ 根據風箏上標示的顏色代號，把風箏填上顏色。

B = blue
R = red
Y = yellow
O = orange
P = pink
G = green
PU = purple
W = white
BL = black
BR = brown

1

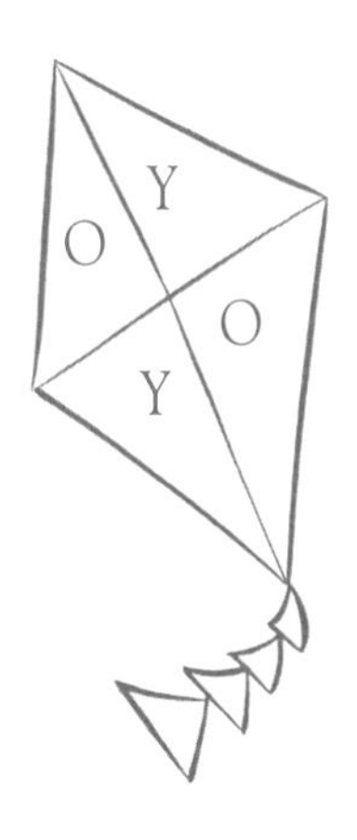

2.

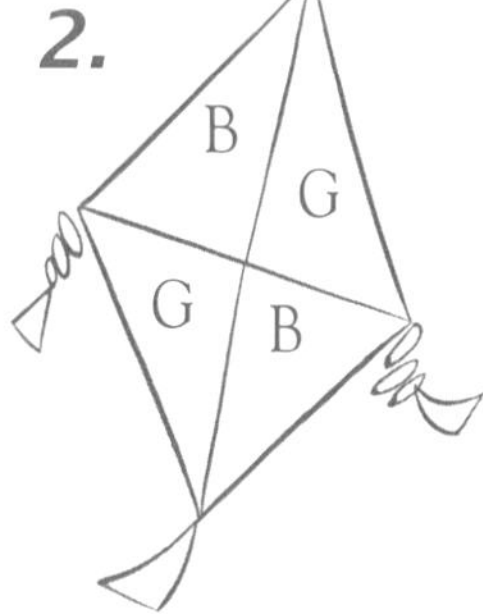

3.

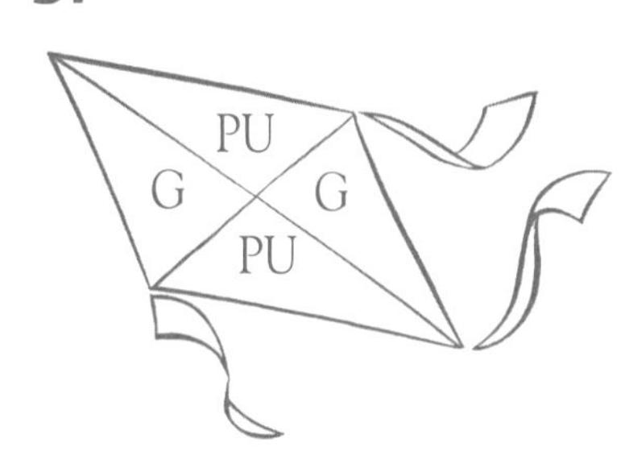

4.

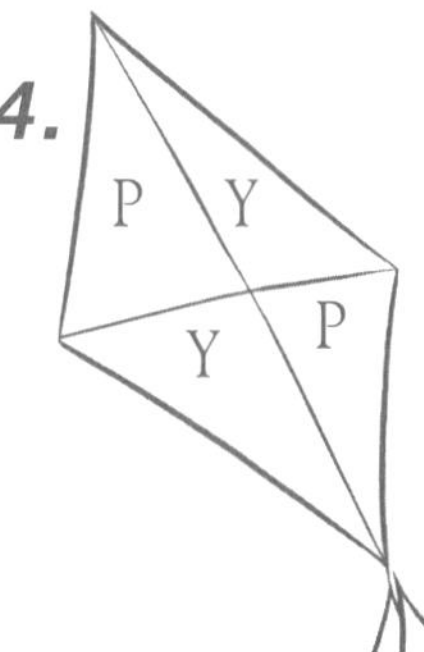

5.

6.

BALLS 皮球

✪ 下面的箱子裏分別有皮球多少個？在箱子上用阿拉伯數字寫出正確的數量，然後在橫線上用英語寫出來。你還可以把皮球填上你喜歡的顏色。

例：

five

1\.

____

2\.

____

3\.

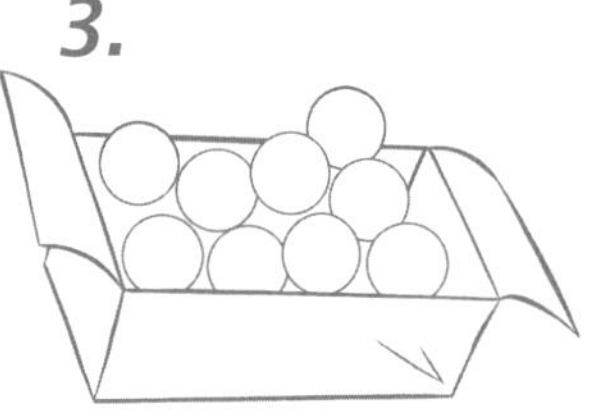

____

4\.

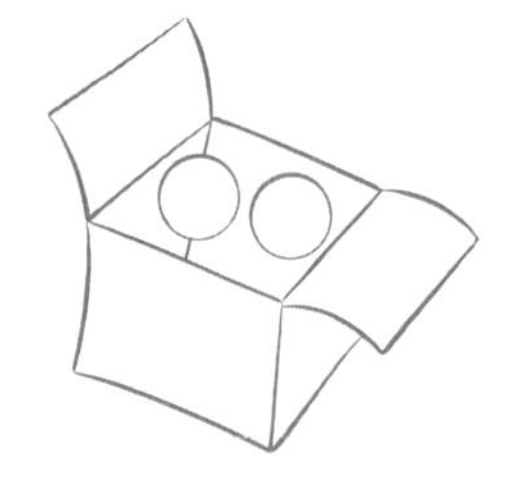

____

5\.

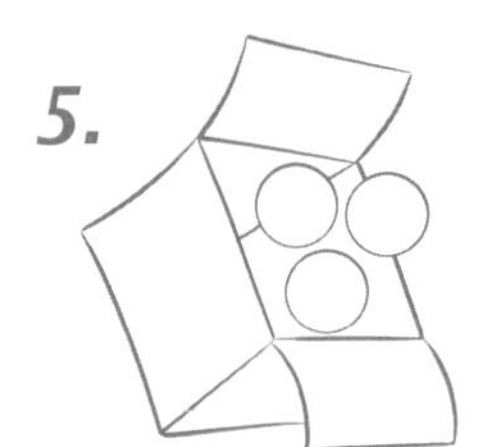

____

6\.

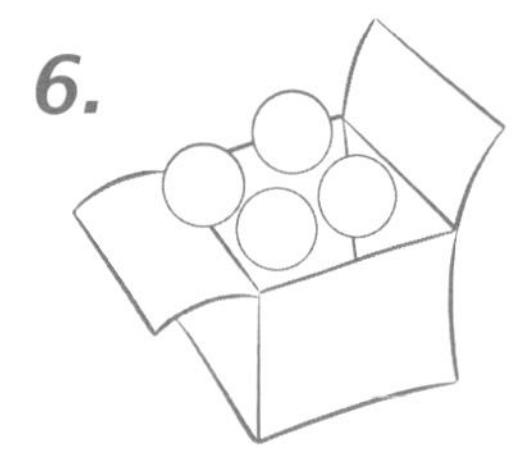

____

7\.

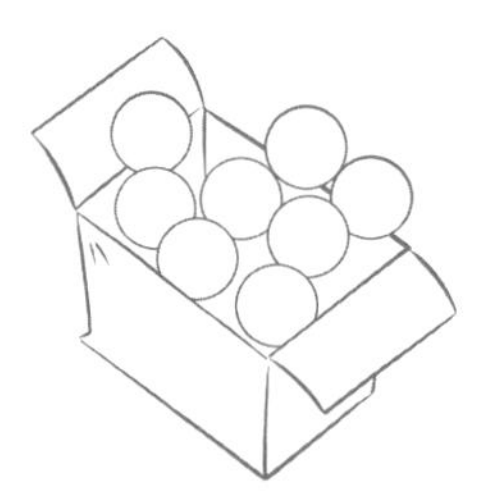

____

8\.

____

9\.

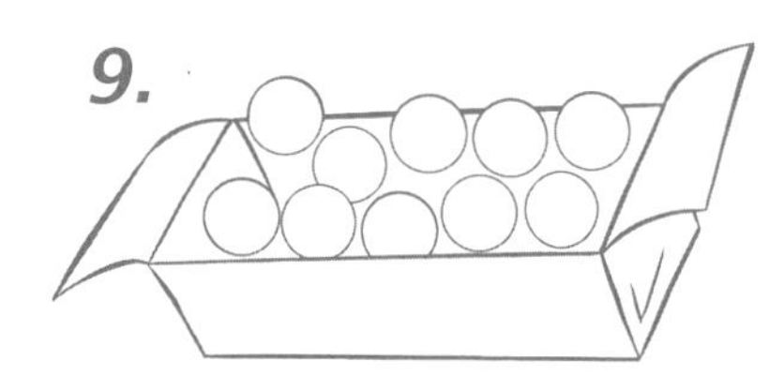

____

NUMBERS 1-10　數字1-10

✪ 根據下面各圖旁邊的文字，每幅圖分別欠了玩具多少件？用英語說說看。

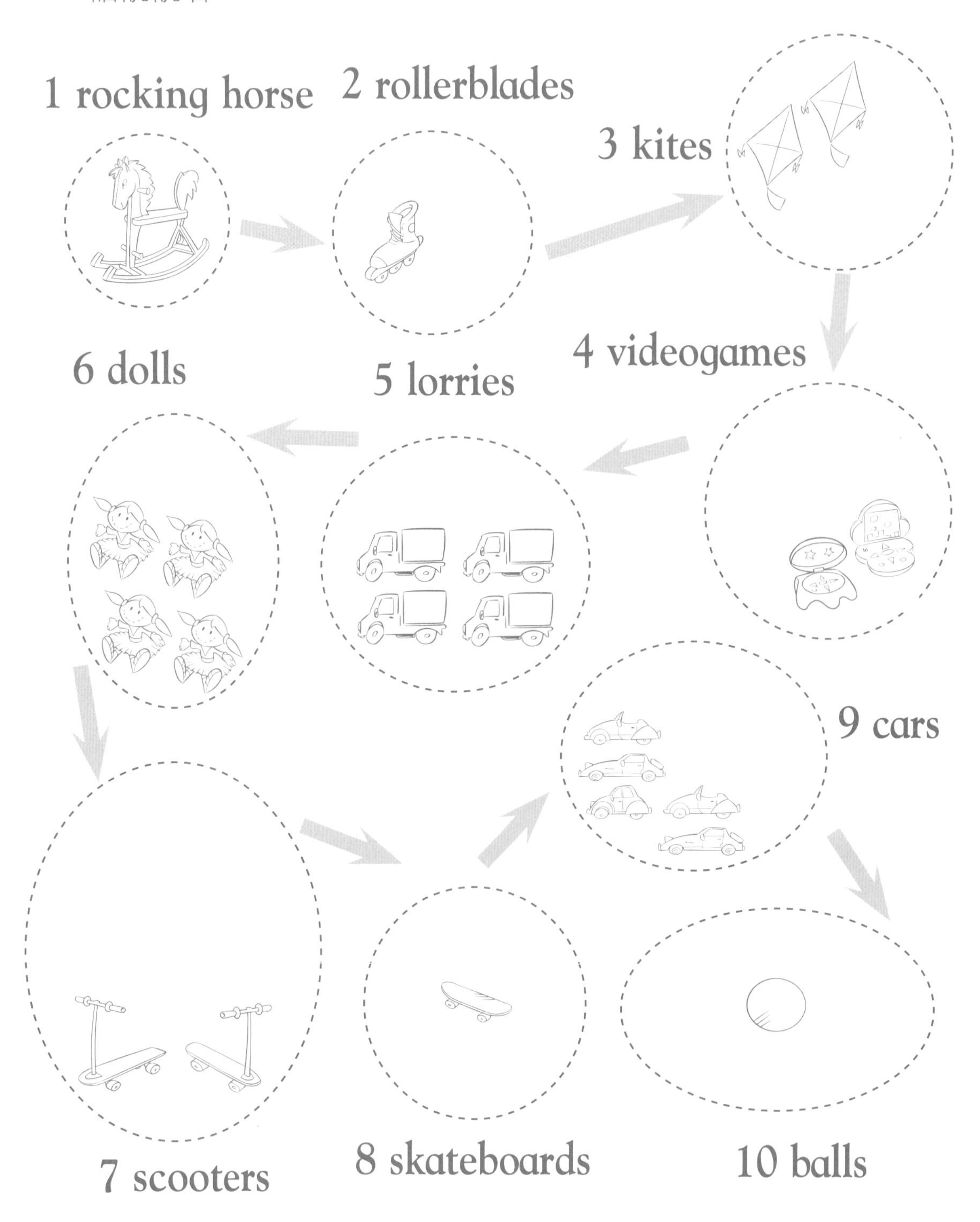

WHAT ARE THEY SAYING?
他們在說什麼？

✪ 仔細看看下面的圖畫，猜猜菲、賴皮、班哲文和潘朵拉在說什麼，根據提示，把適當的字母填在話框裏。

提示：

A. My three teddy bears! B. Hello!
C. My seven cars! D. Hi, Tea!

ANSWERS 答案

TEST 小測驗

1. plane, train, kite, lorry, skipping rope
2. green, orange, blue, red, yellow, pink
3. my ball, my doll, my rollerblades, my toy
4. two, five, three, eight
5. a. My ball is red. b. My scooter is yellow.
   c. My rollerblades are blue. d. My train is green and yellow.

EXERCISE BOOK 練習冊

P.1

1. car 2. lorry 3. bicycle 4. scooter

P.2

1. kite 2. skateboard 3. teddy bear 4. rocking horse 5. plane

P.3

略

P.4

略

P.5

1. six 2. one 3. nine 4. two 5. three 6. four 7. eight
8. seven 9. ten

P.6

各圖中分別欠了玩具如下：
one rollerblade, one kite, two videogames, one lorry, two dolls,
five scooters, seven skateboards, four cars and nine balls

P.7

菲：B 賴皮：D 班哲文：C 潘朵拉：A